ALFIE'S FIRST FIGHT

In 2020 Stories Of Care Founder Sophie Willan invited Children's Author Oliver Sykes to become Stories Of Care's second Lead Artist.

Throughout 2021-22, Oliver collaborated with a handful of exceptional artists to bring this story to life.

This book will be distributed to Looked After Children and children from low-income, single parent backgrounds across the UK, providing an entertaining read that will comfort and inspire.

The creation of *Alfie's First Fight* would not have been possible without the generous support of:

ALFIE'S FIRST FIGHT

PUBLISHED BY

Manchester
Metropolitan
University

WRITTEN BY
OLIVER SYKES

Published in paperback in Great Britain by
Manchester Children's Book Festival
Manchester Metropolitan University
&
Stories Of Care
Copyright © 2022
www.mcbf.org.uk
www.storiesofcare.co.uk

First edition published in May 2022

A CIP record of this book is available from the British Library

Text © Oliver Sykes

Illustrations © Ian Morris

Designed by Sara Merkaj

Cover design by Ian Morris

Printed and bound in England by Manchester Metropolitan University

ISBN: 978-1-910029-74-9

This book is dedicated to my dad,

Christopher Derek Sykes,

And all the other single-parent superheroes out there doing it solo,

Wear your capes proudly!

With love,

Oliver x

ALFIE'S FIRST FIGHT

The biggest fight of our lives is due to start in a boxing ring, in the town hall, in five minutes.

But we've got no **boxer.**

In our family, my big brother Jacob is the boxer, but he isn't here and no one knows where he is.

Behind a thick red curtain that separates Dad and me from the

packed town hall, Dad is pacing up and down, muttering rude words under his breath.

"Son of a gun! Pffft! Un-be-pigging-lievable!"

I'm... distracted.

I can't help thinking about the last time I was here in the town hall.

It was five years ago. I came here to watch a Storyteller with Jacob, Dad and my mum.

Mum loved stories.

It was a happy time... when Mum was still with us.

"Oi! Alfie!" says Dad. "Get your head out of the clouds. We need to find Jacob." He shoots me a look of concern and then looks away. "Oh," he groans. "I do hope he's okay."

Dad is Jacob's boxing coach. Dad used to be a world-boxing champion. Now, he runs his own boxing gym, called Offerle Amateur Boxing Club where he teaches hundreds of upcoming boxers, including me.

One day, I want to be a boxing star like my dad, but he says I'm too young.

I told him. "Dad, I want to be a boxing star."

But he said, "All in good time, Alfie. All in good time. For now, we need to focus on Jacob."

But what good's that when Jacob's not here?

I notice a shaft of light seeping through a tiny hole in the thick red curtain, so I crouch down low, press my right eye against it, and begin to search the crowd.

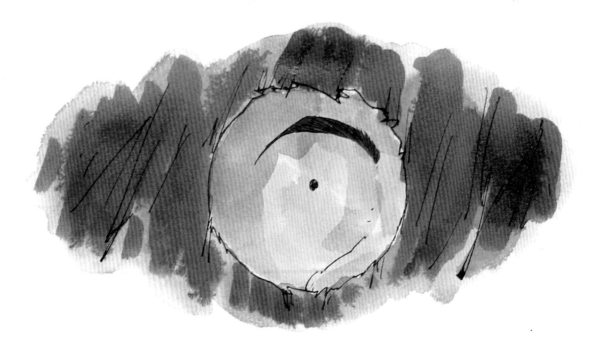

"Eh up!" I mutter to Dad. "There's a girl with blonde pigtails over there, picking her nose. Yikes!" Then, I spot something else. "A boy in a lilac T-shirt scratching his bottom. Yuk! ... And what's that? Huh! Two grown-ups having a snog! Urgh! Get a room!"

Dad says, "Oi! Stop messin'! Where's Jacob? He knows how important this **PRIZE-MONEY** is. Can you see him?"

"Er, not yet," I reply.

"Well, what can you see?"

"Well, aside from all the nose picking, bum-scratching and tonsil tennis out there, it's busy, Dad... lots of people... the ref's in the

ring... the judges are there... and huh! There's a man smoking a cigar! – **smoking a cigar!?** - He can't do that! Oh, wait. No, no, the ref's making him put it out. He doesn't look too happy. In fact, it looks like he's leaving... Sorry Dad. I can't see Jacob anywhere."

Suddenly,

People on the other side of the curtain turn their heads to locate the source of the awful racket. I do the same.

It's Dad.

He's hammering his bare fists against the wall.

"For crying out loud," he bursts. **"where the *heck* is he?"**

Just then, on the other side of the curtain, music starts.

I press my right eye to the hole once more.

At the far end of the hall, a huge, pale-skinned figure, dressed in the town's signature all-black boxing kit, pops up.

Woah! I gasp. "I hope that's not who I think it is!"

"What? Who? Where?" barks Dad.

"At the far end of the hall. It looks like someone's crossed a Boy with

10

a Giant to create the **ULTIMATE. TEENAGE. WARRIOR!** I think that's Jacob's opponent!"

"What makes you say that?"

"He's making his way to the ring!"

The crowd starts whooping and cheering.

I'm so caught up in Jacob's disappearance, I don't even notice that this boy-giant is alone; usually, a fighter makes their way to the ring with their coaching team, but this gargantuan guy is marching towards the ring all by himself.

Quite suddenly, Dad hangs his head.

"This is it," he sobs, looking up at me with shimmering eyes. "It's over. Everything we've worked for all these years, and all because Jacob won't take this seriously. He knows how much we need this prize-money, Alfie, and he's not here."

It's true: we do need it.

This is the biggest fight of our lives.

It's the **Golden Gloves Championship,** Britain's most prestigious competition for young boxers. And our gym, Offerle Amateur Boxing Club, has worked tirelessly to get here.

Jacob needs to win. It's his lifelong dream to become a world-boxing champion, like Dad. It doesn't make sense for him to just give up like this, not when we're so close.

And it isn't just Jacob who needs this.

Dad needs Jacob to win so he can use the prize-money from the fight to pay off the bank, otherwise we might lose our gym altogether.

Dad, Jacob and me live in a small flat on top of the gym. That means if Dad can't pay off the bank, and we lose our gym, then we'll also lose our home.

Losing our home is what I fear the most.

You see, if we lose our home, and have to move away, I'm scared I'll never see my mum ever again.

Mum doesn't live with us anymore.

In fact, I don't know where she lives.

I haven't even seen my mum in four years...

I'm thinking about all of this as I turn back to my dad and say, "Listen, Dad. Everything's going to be okay. Just stay here. If anybody comes asking where Jacob is, we could tell them... **he's gone for a poo!** That ought to buy us... at least thirty minutes. And in the meantime, I will find Jacob and I will bring him back. I promise."

I whip back the curtain, dart out and skirt
the edges of the town hall until I'm standing in a wide,
deserted corridor.

Suddenly it dawns on me: every second I take now is a
second lost.

I need to find Jacob. And fast.

I throw open each door I come to, pop my head inside
and call his name.

"Jacob...? Jacob...?"

But there's no answer.

In fact, there's no sign of him, or anybody else. Anywhere.

Running along these cold, creepy corridors reminds me of the Garden Maze in Manchester where my mum took me when I was six... when she was still with us.

Prickling with nerves, I bolt down what feels like the twentieth corridor when, with a great jolt of relief, I hear two men talking in hushed tones.

"... we cannot afford mistakes," comes an urgent whisper from around the corner, "because if he gets out –"

I'm just about to call out for help when a deep gravelly voice cuts me short.

"He won't, sir. Trust me. The door's bolted from the outside and the fight's about to start."

Wait a minute. Are these men talking about Jacob's fight?

"Even if he does escape," the gravelly voice resumes, "the boy can't fight. His hand got crushed in the door when he tried to escape, didn't it? Ha! Ha! Ha!"

I stifle a gasp.

They are talking about Jacob. They must be. And, he's hurt.

Their voices and footsteps grow louder and louder, and I know then that I have to hide, but I can't. Suddenly, I'm frozen with fear, trying desperately to lift my legs, but they won't budge.

"Come on, legs!" I scold. "Move! Ohhh! Come on! Look, you've got two options: stay frozen and be caught or unfreeze and carry me to safety."

17

Thankfully, my legs choose the latter, and just as the tips of each man's toes turn the corner, I dash into a narrow alcove, sink into the shadows and try my best to be invisible.

Suddenly, and without warning, the air takes on a whole new taste; a gross musty smell that almost makes me gag. And then, in a thick cloud of smoke, both men pass just inches from my face.

I'm so scared I'm shaking all over; yet somehow, I muster the courage to lean out of the shadows and watch them both silently.

The first man is the smaller and smarter-dressed of the two. He's probably about the same age as Dad, maybe a bit older. He's standing side-on, so I can't see his whole face, but he's got slicked-back dark hair, a trim beard and posh-looking glasses with silver rims. He's wearing a fancy black tuxedo and wedged between the forefingers of his left hand is... a lit cigar.

It's him! The man from the ring! The smoker!

"Now, you listen to me," he says to the other man, puffing away on his cigar. "We need that prize-money. If Offerle Amateur Boxing Club wins this fight, then I lose. And I do not lose. Understand?"

I clap my hands over my mouth to stop myself from gasping out loud.

Who on earth is this awful man?

I can only see the other man from behind, but one thing is clear: he is **BIG,** like a bear standing on its hind legs, and he's also wearing the town's signature all-black boxing kit.

19

Is he the boy-giant's father…? I begin to wonder, but the question is soon flung from my mind, as he says, "Trust me, Sir. You've nothing to worry about."

Then, **the posh man** and **THE BIG MAN** disappear through a door, heading back towards the town hall. Suddenly, I feel a strange burning sensation in the pit of my stomach… **FEAR.**

But it isn't just fear.

It's like a cocktail of fear, anger and adrenaline all mixed together.

My **jaw** is **LOCKED SHUT.**

My **fists** are **CLENCHED TIGHT.**

I want to charge after these men and box their ears, but the truth is, I couldn't reach their ears, even if I was standing on a chair.

Besides, I'm no boxer. Not really. Not like Jacob…

"Jacob!" I gasp, coming to my senses.

What on Earth am I thinking!? I have to stop wasting time and get a move on! I have to find him!

I stagger out of my hiding place and begin to pace in the direction the two men have come, turning left and right, and right again, another left, down seemingly endless corridors, calling Jacob's name as loudly as I dare.

As I turn a corner, I almost knock over a fire extinguisher.

The last thing I want to do right now is to make a whopping great clatter by knocking over a fire extinguisher.

"Phew," I say, mopping the sweat from my brow.

Then, I hear something in the distance.

"Jacob...?" I shout, but there's no response.

Every second that passes feels like a stab of pain in the pit of my stomach.

I wonder whether I ought to turn back and tell Dad what I've seen. But then I hear it again.

I can't help but run towards the noise.

Then, I spot a door, on which there's a shiny new padlock.

"Jacob?" I call out.

"Alfie? Is that you, bro?"

"It's me! It's me!" I burst out loud. "Oh gosh, I can't believe I've found you! But… there's a lock on the door. And… I haven't got the key! Oh no!" I start to panic, turning in circles and flapping my arms. "I don't know what to do! I don't know what to do!"

Then, I see it.

Back the way I've come, at the end of the corridor: the fire extinguisher.

I dash back down and pick it up.

It's very, very heavy but nothing can stop me now.

Before I know it, I'm lifting it high in the air and slamming it down on the lock.

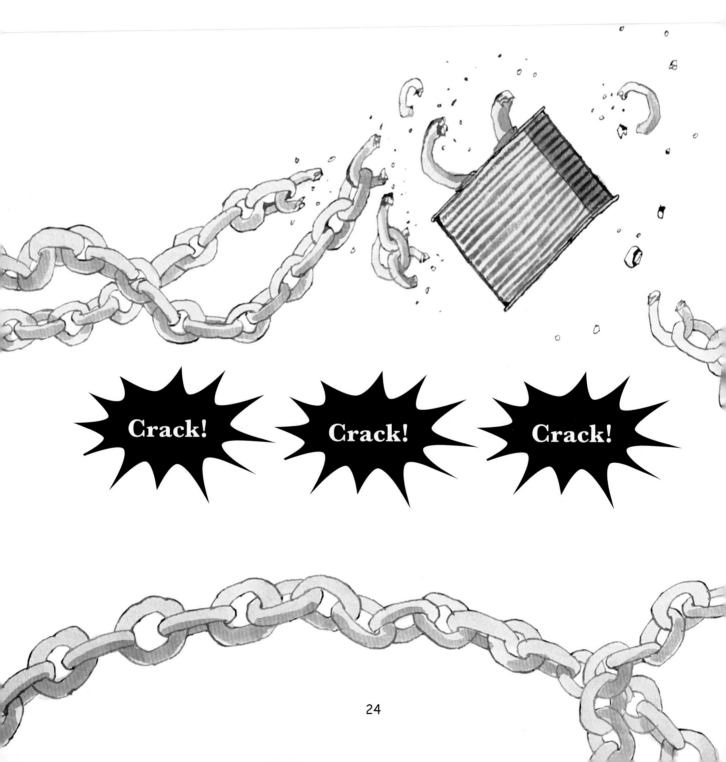

Crack! Crack! Crack!

The lock **bursts.**

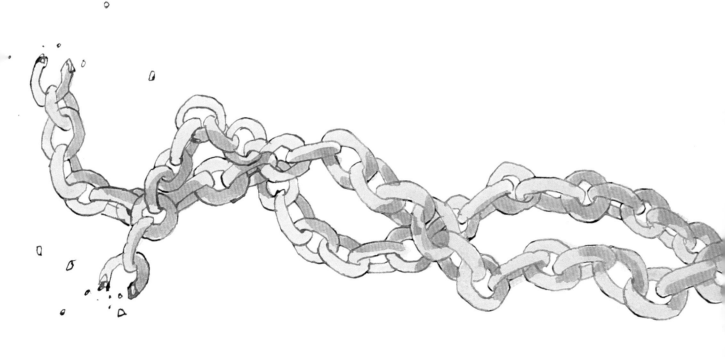

I scramble at the latch and throw open the door.

Whoosh!

There is Jacob.

My eyes immediately fall to his left hand.

Even in the dark, I can see its bad. His middle knuckle is twice its regular size and red all over, and there's a garish purple splotch stretching from his wrist to his thumb. It looks horribly painful.

"Ah mate," says Jacob. "What took you so long?"

"What happened?" I ask, all a tremble.

"Pffft! You tell me," he replies. "One minute, I'm

at the urinal... doing my thing. Next thing I know, some dirt-bag's grabbed me from behind and bashed my head into a wall. After that, I woke up here. I tried to fight my way out but whoever it was smashed the door on my hand and drilled me in. Can you believe it? You know what, I think someone's trying to stop me from winning the fight."

"Too right they are," I say, pulling Jacob out of the closet.

I tell him everything I saw in the corridor.

After which, he stands staring into space. He clearly needs more time for it all to sink in, but unfortunately, time is the one thing we don't have.

"Listen," I say, urgently. "We need to get to the fight right now."

"What?" snaps Jacob. "You expect me to fight with just one hand?"

"Maybe?" I mumble.

Jacob looks doubtful.

"You've already weighed in," I say. "You're already dressed. I can be extra gentle when I'm gloving you up? Dad doesn't have to know."

"But these dirt-bags are cheaters, Alfie. Nah! We need to tell the ref!"

"No! No! Please, Jacob," I beg. "If you tell the ref, he'll call off the fight. We can't afford to lose this fight. If you don't win this fight, and we don't get that prize-money, we'll never see mum again –"

"WHAT HAVE I TOLD YOU ABOUT TALKING TO ME ABOUT HER!?"

Jacob thunders at me; lips shaking, face white, teeth bared, spittle flying in all directions.

All I can do is tremble in fear.

Then…

Cold. Stony. Awkward. Silence.

I don't know what to say.

Even if I did know what to say, I think I'd be too afraid to say it.

Eventually, Jacob takes a deep breath and says, "Pffft! The fight's probably already been cancelled…?"

"We don't know that," I say, in a tiny voice, sounding just as frightened as I feel. "Please? You can do this."

I can see by the look in Jacob's eyes that he feels guilty for losing his temper.

I wait for him to respond.

Eventually, he shrugs his shoulders and says, "Okay. Let's do it. Which way?"

"Yes, good, great," I say. "This way. Quick. Follow me."

We hurry back as fast as we can, and when we get there, the whole crowd's shouting and booing.

The boy-giant is standing in the ring, shaking his fists.

"Where is this Jacob, lad, eh?" he yells to the crowd. **"I best not catch any of you lot hiding him! You! Are you hiding him? Grrrr! The time-wasting coward!!! As soon as I get my hands on him, I'm gonna destroy him!"**

Meanwhile, poor old Dad's pacing up and down outside the dressing area.

Suddenly, he catches sight of us.

"Oh, Jacob!" he gasps, pulling him into a hug. "You're okay? Thank goodness!"

"It's all good, Dad," says Jacob. "You wait here while I get my gloves on. I'm gonna win this fight."

Inside the dressing room, Jacob scrambles for his gum-shield, while I fix his head-guard and his right-glove. Then, comes the tricky part, the left-glove. The moment I try to slip it over Jacob's hand, he flinches in pain.

"OUCH! NO! NO! NO!"

"Come on, Jacob," I coax, "you can do this!"

For a moment, we stare at each other in silent disagreement.

The front of his vest is damp with sweat and his face is chalk white.

"Okay," he says, taking a deep breath. "Let's try again. But be gentle!"

I begin trying to force the glove over Jacob's swollen left hand, but before I can even get it over his fingers, he's writhing in pain, making horrible groaning noises.

"ARGH! ARGH! ARGHHHH! – NO!"

he bursts out, withdrawing his hand. "I can't! I'm sorry, Alfie! I can't do it! It's too painful!"

Just then, in comes Dad.

His eyes fall to Jacob's left hand and his jaw drops.

"What the –? How the –? No! No! No!"

He walks forward and wraps his arms around Jacob. "What happened?" he wails.

"I'm sorry, Dad," Jacob replies. "I only nipped for a quick wee, but –"

"But what?"

"Someone got him, Dad," I shout, unable to stop myself from crying.

Dad looks up. "What do you mean, 'Someone got him'?"

"Someone attacked him. A man. No, two men. But Dad, you have to listen. Every second we spend chatting now is a second lost. That's what these attackers want: for us to waste time and forfeit the fight. Because they're after the prize-money!"

"**WHAT!?**" blasts dad.

Jacob tries to calm him down. He says, "Look, the way I see it, we've got no choice but to tell the ref. It's either that or –"

"Or what?" asks Dad.

For a moment, there's silence.

Deep inside my chest, I feel a small ball of fire beginning to grow.

"I COULD DO IT!" I say.

Again. Silence.

Dad and Jacob exchange a glance and then turn to look at me. "You?" says Dad. "No, Alfie. That lad in the ring is two years older than you, and two stones heavier than you, and this is the Golden Gloves Championship. You're not ready."

"Yes, I am," I say. "I've sparred with Jacob before loads of times. Come on, Dad. Please let me. I can do it."

Jacob says, "Hold on a second. Dad, you've seen Alfie and me sparring before... He's quick on his feet... I actually reckon he could do this... Besides, what choice do we have?"

Before I know it, I'm clad from head to toe in Jacob's shorts, vest, head-guard and gloves.

Dad's jaw drops. "Well, I'll be," he says. "I can hardly tell the difference."

"This is going to work," says Jacob, nodding excitedly.

Just then, in comes Stacey, a woman who helps Dad to run the boxing club.

She's red in the face and gasping for breath. She looks like she's just fought ten rounds herself. She stares at us, eyes wide with fear, and says, "Listen lads… I hate to interrupt but… the ref says if Jacob's not in the ring…in the next thirty seconds… this fight is over!"

Stacey hasn't even noticed that Jacob and me have switched places.

A second later, she's gone.

"Right, Alfie!" says Dad. "This boy is much, much bigger than you, so you need to stay the heck out of his way. Use your speed. Stick and move. Try and get as many clean punches in as possible, but don't risk getting too close. Just get through the first round and we'll talk you through the rest. Okay?"

"Okay."

The next thing I know, the thick red curtain is being pulled back and I'm stepping into the town hall. Immediately, blinding lights and jeering voices stun me. It takes a second for my eyes and ears to adjust, but when they do, I find myself trapped under the glare of several hundred hostile faces.

As I make my way towards the ring, someone shouts,

"TIME-WASTER!"

Another punches the air and shouts,

"YOU CHICKEN!"

Then, a bunch of rowdy men start flapping their arms and clucking at me – like chickens!

"BOK! BOK, BOK, BOK. BOK!"

"Ignore them," shouts Dad, as I fling my leg over the lowest rope and climb up into the ring.

I nod a quick apology to the referee, and then I stand in the corner.

Nobody has noticed mine and Jacob's 'switcheroo' ... or so I think.

The moment I see the men from the corridor, my stomach drops to the floor. The posh man and the big man are both standing ringside, staring up at me in shock. Then, they point right at me and they begin to laugh. **"HA!HA!HA! HA!HA!"**

Quite suddenly, an old memory rises to the surface of my mind.

Right now, right before the first round, right before facing the boy-giant, right at the most crucial moment, I start thinking about... **my mum.**

 *Bang!*

The front door slams shut.
Mum. Gone.
No hugs. No kisses. No goodbyes.
Just... gone.

A sudden sound snaps me back into the present moment.

"Ding! Ding! Ding!"

The bell rings for round one.

The boy-giant charges at me like an angry buffalo.

I break to the right, ducking a huge left hook.

I dash to the left, ducking a huge right hook.

"Come on, Alfie!" barks Dad.

"Fight back!" shouts Jacob.

But I can't think about 'fighting back' right now. All I can do is dip, and dodge and dance. I keep

moving, trying to keep as much distance between the boy-giant and me as possible, but already my legs are beginning to tire, and he's starting to close me down. For a split-second, I stop moving, so I can mop the sweat from my brow, but the moment I do, I hear a great explosion of shouts from behind me.

"Charge!" comes the gravelly voice of the big man.

"What are you waiting for?" shrieks the posh man. There's just enough time for me to register an evil glint in the boy-giant's eyes as he cuts me off to the left and shoves me towards his corner.

I stagger backwards and **skid** on something *slippery.*

I
HIT
THE
CANVAS

Instantly, my head is searing with pain.

When I open my eyes, I'm laying on my side, facing the posh man and the big man. I spot the posh man slip a tin of grease into his jacket pocket.

"Huh!"

The posh man and **THE BIG MAN** greased the canvas.

They are cheating dirt-bags!

The referee starts to count. "One! Two! Three!"

"Are you nuts, ref!?" shouts Dad.

"That was a slip!" shouts Jacob.

"Never!" the posh man roars across the ring. His expression is one of shock and innocence, but my eyes linger just long enough on his face to catch a twist of triumph in his lips.

"Seven," the referee continues. "Eight."

If he counts all the way to ten, the whole thing is over!

"Nine –"

Just then, I hear  **"Ding! Ding! Ding!"**

The bell rings for the end of round one. I struggle to my feet, head throbbing from where it hit the canvas, little stars exploding here, there and everywhere.

Dad helps lower me onto my stool and says, "Alfie, are you all right?"

"Yes, Dad," I say. **"Trust me, I'm gonna win this prize-money. Then you won't have to worry about money. We won't have to move away and I'll see Mum again. We'll all be together."**

Before Dad can reply,

"Ding! Ding! Ding!"

The bell rings for round two.

The boy-giant starts showing off to the crowd, and then, he beckons me closer. I approach with great caution, light as a feather on the balls of my feet, ready to spring away at the earliest sight of danger. I step in; fire a solid jab into his stomach, and retreat before he can react. Once. Twice. Three times.

Knowing I've scored enough points to win the round, I back away, ready to dip and dodge and dance once more, but instantly I know I've been too obvious about it, because my sudden retreat has an effect on the boy-giant like that of pouring petrol on a bomb-fire. His dark eyes pop and he rushes forwards, throwing a devastating punch with all his weight behind it. The punch misses my nose by inches only for the sharpest point of his elbow to strike my chin.

For a moment, everything goes dark and silent.

Dad is mid-way through a cry of horror when I come to.

All I can see are stars.

My head is searing with pain.

Jacob is shouting every foul word under the sun, as a chorus of scandalized groans fills the town hall.

Then,

The bell rings but I don't know what it means.

Have I been knocked out?

Has the ref stopped the fight?

Is it over?

Then, Dad cheers, "The ref's deducting a point!"

"About time," scorns Jacob.

I clamber to my feet, but as I do, I find I'm dizzy, and not the slightly wobbly kind, but the kind that sends the lights swooping around overhead and causes the floor to move in great waves beneath your feet.

There isn't just one boy-giant facing me, but **three!**

The referee gently maneuvers me towards our corner where I slump on my stool, dizzy and dazed.

46

Then, Dad's eyes swim before my own.

"Look up for me, Alfie. Look into my eyes, mate."

I do as he says.

"Listen, it's wonderful that you want to fight for us, but you don't have to. Even without the prize-money, I promise I'll make sure you boys are okay."

"But I'm fighting for Mum too," I say. "I can do this, Dad. I can do this."

"Hey! Look over there," interrupts Jacob, pointing at the opposite corner.

The boy-giant's big barrel of a chest is rising and falling rapidly, along with his massive arms.

"He's only fought two rounds," says Jacob, "but he looks like he's fought ten. He definitely won the first round, but Alfie definitely won the second round, so that means everything now rests on the third and final round. If you can just get out there and stay on your feet, Alfie, you can win this. One more round and it's yours!"

The referee's face swims into view.

"Are you fit to continue?" he asks.

I look from Dad to Jacob. Their eyes are full, as they always have been, with fire and nerve and faith in me.

I shoot the referee a nod and rise to my feet.

Dad's hand settles on my shoulder.

I feel his strength flowing into me.

I'm Alfie Shields, I tell myself. *And win or lose, I'm fighting for my family.*

I stride to the center of the ring, and touch gloves with the boy-giant.

"Ding! Ding! Ding!"

The bell rings for the third and final round.

The crowd explodes with encouragement.

It all comes down to this.

Whoever wins this final round will win the prize-money and the Golden Gloves Championship.

Second by second, I feel my strength returning.

Soon, I'm dancing on the tips of my toes and flicking out my jab, all the while, being very careful to avoid the spot where the posh man and the big man greased the canvas.

Wait a minute, I think to myself. **What if I can get the boy-giant to stumble into his own trap?**

Then, I realize exactly what I have to do...

I take a tactical step back towards the boy-giant's corner and taunt him by sticking out my tongue.

Next, I shout,

"Come and get me, you cheating dirt-bag!"

Then, I turn around and wiggle my
bum at him.

"Na! Na! Na! Na! Na!"

Just as I expect, he takes the bait
and charges forwards.

Just in the nick of time, I leap out
of the way.

The boy-giant hurtles past.

I hear a  followed by a **Bang!**

The posh man shouts, *"No! My PRIZE-MONEY"*

The big man shouts, **"No! My idiot son!"**

Sprawled out on the canvas, the boy-giant cries out,

"I bruised my bum!"

The boy-giant tries to scramble back onto his feet, but before he can, the referee has counted all the way from one to ten.

That's it.

THE FIGHT IS OVER.

"Ding! Ding! Ding!"

WE'VE WON! WE'VE WON!

Dad whisks me up into the air.

I look out at the crowd, all of who are standing on their feet, clapping.

The tingly magic of winning rushes through me like electricity.

Jacob yells, "You did it, bruv!"

Dad shouts, "Hooray!"

There and then, I realize...

If this fight has taught me **one thing**, *it's this:*

Mum isn't here right now, and that is sad, but you know what?

It's okay.

Because I've got Dad and I've got Jacob.

And we've all got each other.

That is the **GREATEST PRIZE** *of all.*

THE END

Praise for Alfie's First Fight

'Alfie's First Fight isn't just an amazing story about boxing: it's about love, loss, family and how to fight for what you want; a must-read for any plucky youngster.' **SOPHIE WILLAN**

'A positive and gripping story for kids about a young man and his journey into the world of boxing. With highs and lows along the way, it captures the true drama of the boxing ring.' **RICKY HATTON**

'It's so rare to come across a working-class narrative that portrays a single father raising his children. Alfie's First Fight is not just about the struggles of a young man approaching his first fight in the ring, but the wider battle for the working class of being validated, accepted and taking their place in society.' **ALEX WHEATLE**

'Alfie's First Fight not only captures what it is like to be a boxer and step into the ring with all the nerves and adrenaline that comes with it; but also acknowledges the real struggle of working-class families, of single parents, and the special love and bond which comes from those experiences.' **STACEY COPELAND**

'Hugely relatable for any child who's had a dream they'd do anything to achieve.' **DOMINIC BERRY**

'A positive story for small kids and big kids, alike. If Alfie continues with his career, he could well become a People's Champion and a World Boxing Champion, just like Frank!' **THE FRANK BRUNO FOUNDATION**

'This punchy, action-packed story had me hooked from the start. It's David and Goliath with boxing gloves!' **JENNY MOORE**

'A great read, showing how anything is possible with hard work, dedication and support; a true reflection of a boxer's dream.' **NIGEL TRAVIS, MOSS SIDE FIRE STATION BOXING CLUB**